I0582928

OUTCAST MAGIC

Laura Shenton

OUTCAST MAGIC

Laura Shenton

Iridescent Toad Publishing

Iridescent Toad Publishing.

©Laura Shenton 2025
All rights reserved.

Laura Shenton asserts the moral right to be identified as the author of this work.

No part of this publication may be
reproduced, stored or transmitted in any form or by any means, electronic, mechanical, photocopying, recording, scanning, or otherwise without written permission from the publisher. It is illegal to copy this book, post it to a website, or distribute it by any other means without permission.

This book is entirely a work of fiction. The names, characters and incidents portrayed in it are the work of the author's imagination. Any resemblance to actual persons, living or dead, events or localities is entirely coincidental.

Designations used by companies to distinguish their products are often claimed as trademarks. All brand names and product names used in this book and on its cover are trade names, service marks, trademarks and registered trademarks of their respective owners. The publishers and the book are not associated with any product or vendor mentioned in this book. None of the companies referenced within the book have endorsed the book.

Cover by Janina Cover Designs.

First edition. ISBN 978-1-913779-13-9

Chapter One

The ancient stones of the graveyard loomed around Jeanette, their weathered faces barely visible in the night. Centuries-old monuments to the departed stood as silent sentinels, their intricate carvings worn smooth by time and the elements. Ornate angelic figures, no longer pristine and comforting, seemed to leer at her with hollow eyes and rictus grins.

As she huddled against a crumbling mausoleum, its once-grand façade now a patchwork of moss and decay, Jeanette's pale skin was bright against the darkness, setting her apart from the shadows that danced and shifted around her. Her long dark hair, usually so carefully tended with herbal tonics and gentle magic, hung in damp, tangled strands around her face. Each breath she exhaled sent wisps of fog curling into the air, a physical manifestation of the chill that had settled deep within her bones. She drew her cloak tighter, its fabric rough against her skin. The garment, once a source of pride and a symbol of her craft, now served as a meagre shield against the biting cold and the weight of her newfound solitude.

Jeanette's eyes, normally attuned to reading the subtlest shifts in magical energies, strained to make out the shapes of the tombstones surrounding her. In this place of endings, despite her instincts as a witch, her senses felt dulled, smothered by the oppressive silence and the lingering miasma of decay.

This place of the dead had become her sanctuary, a bitter irony that wasn't lost on her. The graveyard's sepulchral silence enveloped her like a shroud, broken only by the occasional rustle of dead leaves skittering across weathered stone or the mournful hoot of a distant owl. These sounds, once eerie reminders of mortality, now offered a strange comfort in their familiarity.

A profound sense of loss weighed heavily upon Jeanette as she thought about all she had left behind. She had always viewed her magic as a gift, a means to help and heal, to bring light into the darkest corners for those in need. Now, that same power had made her an outcast, forced to seek refuge among the dead because the living had turned against her. The injustice of it all threatened to overwhelm her usually calm demeanour.

As if in sympathy with her tumultuous emotions, the sky opened up, releasing a steady, cold rain. Droplets pelted the stone markers and Jeanette's huddled form, quickly soaking through her cloak. The rain traced rivulets down the faces of nearby statues, creating the illusion of weeping angels mourning her plight. She didn't bother to cast a spell to keep herself dry; the effort seemed pointless in the face of her current predicament. Instead, she allowed the rain to mingle with the tears she had been holding back, grateful for the chance to release her sorrow without feeling wholly vulnerable.

Her thoughts wandered back to the events that had led her here, each memory as sharp and painful as the rocks that had been hurled at her. Millbrook, the town she had called home for so long, now seemed like a distant dream. Its warm hearths and friendly faces had been replaced by a nightmare of fear and hatred. In her mind's eye, she replayed the faces of people she had once considered friends, and how their expressions had become contorted with fear and anger. Their gazes, previously filled with gratitude for her healing touch, had blazed with suspicion and hatred. Children whose ailments she had once soothed had cowered behind their parents' legs, their innocence shattered by the sudden turn of events.

She had tried to reason with everyone, her voice rising above the growing murmur of the crowd. The words she had spoken echoed in her mind, a desperate plea that had fallen on deaf ears. "Please," she had begged, her hands outstretched in a gesture of supplication, "I have only ever used my magic for good! I've healed your sick, protected your crops from blight and pests. I would never curse anyone!" But her words, lost in the cacophony of accusation, had been drowned out by shouts of "Witch!" and "Sorceress!". The clatter of farming tools repurposed as weapons had punctuated cries of anger, a discordant symphony of fear and ignorance.

The rocks they'd hurled at her had knocked

her to the ground. Jeanette winced at the memory, her hand unconsciously moving to her side where a particularly large stone had left a painful bruise. The impact had driven the breath from her lungs, leaving her gasping on the ground when the mob closed in. She had always prided herself on her ability to stay calm in a crisis, to be the steady hand guiding others through difficult times. But in that moment, terror had taken hold.

The scene replayed itself in her mind with brutal clarity: the gathering crowd, their faces twisted with fear and rage; the raised pitchforks glinting ominously in the stormy light, tools meant for harvest now turned to darker purpose; the growing panic as more residents succumbed to the mysterious curse that had befallen the town. Jeanette remembered the horror she'd felt when a small group of the cursed population had suddenly bolted into the forest, their bodies contorting in ways that defied natural law. Limbs had elongated grotesquely, skin had rippled and shifted like water, and beastly cries had torn from throats no longer wholly human. They had vanished into the shadows of the trees, beyond her reach before she could even attempt to help them.

As Jeanette shifted uncomfortably against the cold stone of the mausoleum, she found herself at a loss. The question of where to go from here loomed as large and imposing as the graveyard monuments surrounding her. Who would take in a witch accused of such terrible deeds? Communities of magic users were scarce, and the journey to reach them would be perilous. A feeling of isolation wrapped around her, cold and unyielding, seeping into her bones like the chill of the rain-soaked cloak draped over her shoulders.

A flicker of doubt crept into her mind, a poisonous tendril threatening to take root. Could she somehow have caused this curse without having realised it? Had her magic, always meant to nurture and protect, somehow twisted into something malevolent? No, she told herself firmly, pushing back against the insidious thought. She knew her craft, knew the precise limits of her powers. This was something else entirely, something far darker than anything she was capable of. The magic behind this curse felt wrong, tainted in a way that made her skin crawl even at the memory.

She recalled the image of something she had

seen, impossible to ignore: the stranger she had glimpsed just before the chaos erupted in the town. There had been something off about them, a wrongness she couldn't quite put her finger on. The stranger had stood at the edge of the town square, observing the daily bustle with an intensity that had made her feel uneasy. Their eyes had met for a brief moment, and she had felt a chill run down her spine. Perhaps it had been a premonition of the disaster to come. Could they have been responsible for the curse?

The thought gave Jeanette pause. She was loath to cast blame without evidence, all too aware of how quickly accusations could spiral out of control. Hadn't she just fallen victim to such hasty judgment herself? Still, the memory of the stranger lingered, refusing to be dismissed.

There had been something undeniably different about them, a quality that set them apart from the usual travellers and merchants who passed through the town. Jeanette closed her eyes, trying to recall every detail. The stranger's gait had been too smooth, almost gliding across the cobblestones. Their clothing, while not outlandish, had seemed oddly out of place, as if belonging to no particular region or style she could name. However, it was their eyes that truly stood out in her memory. Deep-set and intense, they had seemed to absorb the light rather than reflect it.

She shook her head, frustrated. It wasn't enough to go on – certainly not enough to level an accusation. For all she knew, the stranger could have been an innocent traveller, their odd appearance nothing more than a trick of her worried mind.

Yet the timing was troubling. The curse had manifested so soon after the stranger's arrival. Could it truly have been mere coincidence?

Chapter Two

The town of Millbrook, once a haven of tranquillity nestled between rolling hills and ancient forests, now writhed in the grip of a nameless terror. The streets, usually bustling with the cheerful cacophony of daily life, had fallen eerily silent. Shutters remained tightly closed, and doors were barred against the encroaching darkness that seemed to seep from every shadow.

Through this desolate landscape strode a figure that exuded an aura of otherworldly power. The stranger, tall and lithe, moved with a grace that belied his predatory nature. His perfectly tailored suit, a deep midnight blue that seemed to absorb what little light remained, moved elegantly with him as he took each measured step over the cobblestones. His pale skin, smooth as marble, contrasted sharply with the vibrant crimson of his lips, which were curved into a perpetual smirk of cruel amusement.

This was no mere man, but a creature of legend and nightmare – a vampire who had walked the earth for centuries, leaving a trail of broken lives and shattered communities in his wake. Yet there was nothing monstrous about his appearance. He exuded a sophisticated charm, his every gesture calculated to entice and beguile. It was only in his eyes – depthless pools of obsidian – that the true horror lurking beneath the surface could be glimpsed.

As the vampire sauntered down the main street, a small group of townspeople huddled in the shadow of the old clock tower, their voices hushed but urgent. Amongst them was Thomas, the burly blacksmith; Sarah, the town's midwife; and old Mr Fairfax, whose wizened face was creased with worry.

"We've made a terrible mistake," Thomas muttered, his usual confidence shaken. "Jeanette... she couldn't have been behind this curse. Not our Jeanette."

Sarah nodded, wringing her hands anxiously.

"I've known her since she was a mere child," she said. "She's only ever used her magic to help us. Remember when she saved my little Emily from the fever last winter?"

"Indeed," said Mr Fairfax, his rheumy eyes darting nervously. "But if it wasn't Jeanette, then who...?"

His voice trailed off as his gaze settled on the approaching figure of the vampire.

"It's him," Thomas said in a low growl, his fists clenching at his sides. "That stranger. He arrived just before all of this started. And now look at us – cowering in our own town while Jeanette's out there alone, goodness knows where."

"We should have listened to her," Sarah lamented. "She tried to tell us she was innocent, but we were too afraid to hear it. And now..."

Their hushed conference was cut short as the vampire suddenly appeared before them, moving with a speed that defied human perception. His lips curled back in a snarl, revealing gleaming fangs.

"Now, now," he said in a low purr, his voice as smooth as silk and as cold as ice. "It's not polite to speak ill of your betters – especially when they can hear every... little... word."

The group shrank back, terror etched on their faces.

"You seem to have some misguided notion about who's truly in control here," the vampire continued, his eyes glittering with malicious glee. "Perhaps a demonstration is in order."

With a languid gesture, he beckoned to a young man who had been trying to slip away unnoticed. The unfortunate soul found himself unable to resist the vampire's magnetic pull, and, despite his better judgment, his feet reluctantly began to move, drawing him closer to the threat.

"You see," the vampire explained, almost condescendingly, "I have the power to reshape reality itself. Your little witch friend? A mere trickster compared to what I can do. Observe."

He placed a hand on the young man's forehead, and the air around them began to shimmer and warp. The young man's scream of agony was cut short as his body began to twist and contort. Bones cracked and reformed, skin rippled and sprouted coarse fur, and within moments, where once had stood a human now crouched a monstrous beast, its eyes wild with pain and confusion.

The assembled townspeople gasped and cried out in horror, but the vampire merely dusted off his hands, looking supremely unconcerned.

"That's what happens to those who displease me," he said casually. "So I suggest you all remember your place. Unless, of course, you'd like to join your friends in the forest."

Leaving the traumatised group in his wake, the vampire continued his leisurely stroll through the town. He soon came upon a small cottage, its door ajar and interior dark. The faint scent of fear and desperation still lingered in the air – clearly, this had been the home of one of the cursed who had fled into the forest.

With a chuckle, the vampire pushed the door wide open and sauntered inside. He ran a finger along a dusty shelf, tutting at the mess and disorder.

"How quaint," he murmured, settling himself into a worn armchair by the cold fireplace.

With a snap of his fingers, flames roared to life, casting dancing shadows across the room. As he lounged there, a self-satisfied smirk played across his lips. Everything was going according to plan. It had been child's play to plant the seeds of doubt about the witch, Jeanette. Humans were so delightfully predictable in their paranoia and suspicion. With her out of the way, there would be no one to challenge his dominion over this miserable little town.

"Ah, Jeanette," he mused aloud, savouring the name like a fine wine. "Such potential, wasted on healing scrapes and blessing crops. If only you knew the true power that courses through your veins. Never mind – you're gone, and I'm here to stay."

Chuckling to himself again, the vampire closed his eyes, allowing the warmth of the fire and the intoxicating scent of fear permeating through the town to lull him into a contented slumber. As consciousness slipped away, his final thought was of the delicious chaos yet to come.

***

Miles away, deep in the heart of the forest, a very different scene was unfolding. The trees, ancient and gnarled, seemed to lean away from the clearing where the cursed townspeople were gathered. These were no longer the friendly faces of neighbours and friends, but twisted caricatures of humanity. Some crouched on all fours, their limbs elongated and joints bent at unnatural angles. Others stood upright, but their features had become bestial – snouts where noses should be, fur sprouting in patches across their skin, eyes glowing with an unnatural light in the darkness.

They milled about restlessly, occasionally letting out low growls or whimpers of confusion and pain. The curse had robbed them of their ability to speak, but flashes of human consciousness still flickered behind their altered visages. A mother, now more wolf than woman, nuzzled against her equally transformed child. An elderly couple, their bodies now twisted and severely hunched, leaned against each other for support.

At the edge of the clearing, partially obscured by the shadows of the towering trees, stood a figure fully shaped by his beastly transformation. It was the town's former mayor, now teetering on the brink of monstrosity.

He let out a mournful howl. It was quickly taken up by others until the entire forest echoed with their lament – a cry for the humanity they had lost.

As the sound faded, an oppressive silence settled over the cursed souls of Millbrook. They huddled closer together, lost, afraid, and slowly losing touch with everything they had ever known.

Chapter Three

As the night wore on, Jeanette remained huddled in the graveyard, her thoughts as turbulent as the storm that raged around her. The rain, relentless and cold, had long since soaked through her cloak, chilling her to the bone. Exhaustion tugged at her limbs, yet she remained standing, propped against a weathered tombstone, her fingers tracing the worn engravings as if seeking answers from the long-departed.

The young witch found herself at a crossroads, each path before her shrouded in uncertainty. Her home, once a sanctuary of warmth and comfort, was now forbidden to her, guarded by the very people she had sworn to protect. The forests that bordered Millbrook, usually a source of solace and wonder, now seemed foreboding and unwelcoming.

Jeanette tilted her head back, allowing the rain to wash over her face. She closed her eyes, trying to centre herself, to find some spark of inspiration or guidance in the whirlwind of her thoughts. The cool droplets mingled with her tears, a cathartic release that left her feeling hollow yet somehow lighter.

As she opened her eyes, gazing up at the roiling clouds above, something caught her attention: a movement, swift and purposeful, unlike the random patterns of wind-tossed debris. She squinted, her senses prickling with a sudden awareness of something unusual, powerful, and undeniably domineering.

A figure descended from the turbulent sky, its form gradually taking shape as it neared. Jeanette's breath caught in her throat as she realised what she was seeing: a reaper, one of the enigmatic beings tasked with shepherding souls to the afterlife. But this was no skeletal horror like the ones in children's tales. The reaper before her was unmistakeably female, with long black hair cascading down her shoulders like a dark waterfall, her ethereal form draped in flowing robes woven from shadows and starlight.

The reaper came to a halt just above and in front of Jeanette, her presence overwhelming in its sheer otherworldliness. Jeanette found herself unable to look away, her own magic thrumming through her veins in response to the palpable power emanating from the being. Her every instinct screamed that this creature was a threat, a danger to be reckoned with, yet Jeanette stood her ground, summoning what courage she could muster.

"Who are you?" Jeanette called out, her voice shakier than she would have liked. "What do you want with me?"

The reaper's voice, when it came, was surprisingly melodious, carrying hints of distant wind chimes and whispered lullabies:

"I am she who walks between worlds, young witch. And I come bearing news of your home, Millbrook."

"Millbrook?!" Jeanette exclaimed, her heart leaping into her throat. "What's happened? Is everyone alright?"

"Your town has fallen under a curse, cast by a vampire of great malevolence and power," the reaper explained, her form shimmering as if disturbed by an unseen breeze. "He turned the people against you, convincing them that you were the source of their misfortune. By the time they realised the truth, it was too late."

Anger flared within Jeanette, hot and bright against the chill of the rain.

"That monster!" she said furiously. "I knew there was something off about that stranger! And now the whole town is suffering because of him!"

"Your anger is justified, young one," said the reaper, inclining her head in a gesture that seemed to convey both sympathy and approval. "But it can also be a weapon, if wielded correctly. You must return to Millbrook and face this vampire. Only you have the power to break his curse and save the townspeople."

"But how?" Jeanette asked, her mind reeling with the enormity of the task. "I'm just one witch. How can I hope to stand against a vampire powerful enough to curse an entire town?"

"There is a place," the reaper said, her voice taking on an almost conspiratorial tone. "An abandoned library in the next town over. Within its walls, you will find shelter from those who would harm you, and ancient tomes of magic that will teach you the spells needed to defeat this evil. Go there, study, and prepare yourself for the battle to come."

Suspicion crept into Jeanette's thoughts, tempering her initial surge of hope.

"Why are you telling me this?" she asked. "Why would you want to help me? Reapers and witches... we've never exactly been on friendly terms."

A sound like distant rueful laughter emanated from the reaper.

"True enough, young witch. But in this, our interests align. I despise vampires far more than I could ever dislike your kind. This particular individual has gone too far, cursing so many at once. Do you have any idea how much extra work that will create for me?"

Recognising the note of genuine irritation in the reaper's ethereal voice, Jeanette considered the facts. On the one hand, trusting a reaper went against everything she had ever been taught. On the other, she was desperate for shelter, for a chance to reclaim her place in Millbrook, and for the opportunity to right the wrongs inflicted upon the innocent – even if they had accused her.

After a moment's hesitation, Jeanette nodded.

"Alright," she said. "I'll do it. Take me to this library."

"A wise choice," the reaper replied, her form seeming to pulse with satisfaction. "Prepare yourself, young witch. The journey will be... unconventional."

Before Jeanette could ask what that meant, the world around her began to shift and warp. The rainy graveyard dissolved into a swirling vortex of strange patterns and sensations. She felt herself being pulled in every direction at once, her physical form seeming to stretch and compress in ways that should have been impossible.

Fragments of realities flashed by – glimpses of distant stars and swirling nebulae, fleeting images of unfamiliar landscapes populated by shadows beyond comprehension. Jeanette heard whispers in languages never meant for human ears, saw colours that had no names in any earthly tongue.

Time lost all meaning as they traversed the spaces between worlds. Jeanette felt as though she had lived a thousand lifetimes and yet no time at all had passed. Just when she thought she could bear no more, reality snapped back into focus with dizzying abruptness.

Jeanette found herself standing before an imposing structure, its gothic architecture looming against the storm-wracked sky. The abandoned library stood silent and foreboding, yet she could sense the wealth of knowledge and power contained within its weathered walls.

She turned to thank the reaper – with hopes of asking for more guidance – but Jeanette quickly realised she was alone. The ethereal being was already retreating, ascending into the turbulent heavens without a word of farewell.

Chapter Four

As Jeanette stood before the abandoned library, the rain continued its relentless assault, each droplet a bitter reminder of her precarious situation. Despite her uncertainty about this new environment, her immediate needs took precedence. She was grumpy, cold, wet, and bone-weary, her body and mind crying out for shelter and rest.

She gazed up at the imposing structure before her. The library's gothic architecture was unmistakable, with spires and buttresses reaching towards the storm-wracked sky. Gargoyles peered down from their lofty perches, their weathered faces seeming to mock her plight. The building's grandeur, though faded by time and neglect, was still evident in its intricate stonework and towering stained glass windows, now dark and lifeless in the gloom.

Jeanette's eyes darted from one possible entry point to another, hope rising and falling with each observation. Every window appeared to be tightly shut, their panes coated with years of grime. The massive oak doors at the front of the building loomed before her, promising sanctuary but also presenting a formidable barrier.

With a sigh that was part determination and part frustration, Jeanette approached the main entrance. She placed her hands on the ornate handle, its brass surface cold and slick with rain. She pushed, then pulled, then pushed again with all her might. The door remained stubbornly closed, unyielding to her efforts.

"Curse it all," she muttered, her patience wearing thin.

She took a deep breath, forcing herself to be calm. There had to be another way in. She wasn't about to let a mere locked door defeat her, not after all she'd been through.

Steeling herself against the continuing downpour, Jeanette began to circle the building. Her sodden cloak clung to her legs, hampering her progress, but she pressed on. As she rounded a corner, her heart leapt at the sight of a smaller, less ornate side door. It was shut, like all the others, but something about it called to her.

Approaching with cautious hope, she placed her hand on the door's weathered surface. To her immense relief, it swung open with surprising ease, as if welcoming her home. A gust of musty air rushed out to greet her as she stepped over the threshold, leaving the storm behind.

She found herself in a narrow, dimly lit corridor. The air was thick with the scent of old paper and neglect. Cobwebs draped from the ceiling like tattered lace, and a thick layer of dust coated every surface. The floorboards creaked ominously under her feet as she made her way forward, her eyes straining to adjust to the gloom.

As she walked, her mind raced with possibilities. She reasoned that somewhere in this labyrinthine building would be a room where she could rest, where she could begin to make sense of the whirlwind of events that had brought her here. She pressed on, navigating the unfamiliar space with cautious steps, her senses alert for any sign of direction in the dimness.

After what felt like an eternity of navigating twisting corridors and avoiding precariously stacked piles of books, Jeanette finally emerged into a vast, open space. She gasped, momentarily forgetting her exhaustion as she took in the sight before her.

The main library room was a cathedral of knowledge, its vaulted ceiling lost in shadows high above. Towering bookshelves stretched as far as the eye could see, their contents a treasure trove of arcane wisdom. Ornate wrought-iron spiral staircases connected different levels, their steps worn smooth by countless feet over the centuries. Massive chandeliers hung suspended, their crystals dull with neglect but still hinting at former glory.

In the centre of the room was a grand reading area, dominated by long tables of dark, polished wood. High-backed chairs, their upholstery faded and torn, were arranged haphazardly around the space. Jeanette's eyes were drawn to the far wall, where an enormous fireplace stood cold and empty, flanked by intricately carved stone griffins.

As she moved further into the room, Jeanette's gaze fell upon the books themselves. Even in the low light, she could make out titles that made her thoughts race with excitement and trepidation: 'Compendium of Vampiric Weaknesses', 'Advanced Defensive Spellcraft', 'Curses and Their Countermeasures' – tomes that promised the very knowledge she would need to save her town and defeat the vampire who had caused so much suffering.

But as enticing as the books were, Jeanette's exhaustion reasserted itself with a vengeance. Her limbs felt like led, and her eyelids drooped despite her best efforts to stay alert. With a reluctant sigh, she turned her attention to creating some semblance of a bed.

She gathered what she could find: a faded tapestry from the wall, and cushions from various chairs. She arranged her finds in a relatively clear space near one of the bookshelves, creating a nest that, while far from luxurious, would at least keep her off the cold floor.

As she settled onto her improvised bed, Jeanette's mind whirled with the events of the day: the reaper's otherworldly presence, the vampire's cruel deception, the painful memory of her neighbours having turned against her. All of it swirled in an upsetting jumble. Questions and worries nagged at her: How would she learn the magic needed to defeat a vampire? Would she be able to break the curse on her town? What if she failed?

Yet, despite the tumult of her thoughts, Jeanette could no longer ignore her exhaustion. Her eyes grew heavy, the world around her blurring. In mere moments, she slipped into a deep sleep, her last conscious thought a determination to face whatever challenges tomorrow might bring.

As Jeanette slept, the library stood still around her. The ancient books, witnesses to centuries of human striving and magical endeavours, seemed to watch over the young witch. In the quiet of the night, the only sound was the distant patter of rain against the windows.

Chapter Five

The abandoned library lay silent in the early hours of the morning as the first rays of dawn began to filter in through the dusty windows. Jeanette, exhausted from her ordeal, slept fitfully on her makeshift bed. Her dreams were an unpleasant blend of swirling shadows, accusing faces, and the haunting laughter of a vampire she had yet to confront. In her mind's eye, she imagined the terrifying individual who had brought such misery to her hometown – eyes glowing red with unholy hunger, fangs glinting in the moonlight.

Suddenly, a piercing scream shattered the stillness, jolting Jeanette from her uneasy slumber. Her heart pounding furiously, she bolted upright, her eyes wide with shock and confusion. The scream, so unexpected in this place of quiet contemplation, awakened memories of the angry mob that had driven her from her home. For a moment, she feared that they had somehow found her, that her brief respite in this forgotten place was at an end.

As Jeanette's sleep-addled mind struggled to make sense of her surroundings, her gaze landed on the source of the disturbance. Standing just a few feet away, equally startled, was a young woman who, like Jeanette, appeared to be in her early twenties. The young woman's long blonde hair cascaded over her shoulders, framing a face that, despite its current expression of shock, was undeniably pretty. She was dressed in long black robes, with a smart red jumper visible beneath. She clutched a stack of ancient-looking books to her chest, as if they might shield her from whatever danger she had perceived.

"Oh my goodness, I'm so sorry!" the young woman exclaimed remorsefully, her words tumbling out in a rush as her cheeks flushed with embarrassment. "I didn't mean to frighten you. I'm Heidi. I come here to study, and I was just so surprised to see someone else. I've never encountered anyone here before."

Jeanette's initial fear began to subside as she took in Heidi's appearance and demeanour. Despite her lingering grogginess and a twinge of annoyance at having been so rudely awakened, Jeanette could sense no malice from the other woman. After the hostility and betrayal she had experienced in her hometown, the presence of someone who seemed kind was a welcome change.

"It's... it's alright," Jeanette managed, her voice still rough with sleep as she ran a hand through her tangled hair, trying to make herself look somewhat presentable. "I'm Jeanette. I only arrived here last night."

Heidi's face softened with sympathy as she took in Jeanette's dishevelled appearance.

"I hope you don't think I'm being rude," she said gently, "but you look absolutely exhausted. Have you eaten anything? I always bring coffee and sandwiches with me when I come here for long study sessions. Would you like some?"

The mention of food made Jeanette suddenly aware of the gnawing emptiness in her stomach.

"That would be wonderful," she said gratefully. "Thank you."

As Heidi busied herself with retrieving the offered refreshments from her bag, Jeanette took the opportunity to stretch and properly wake up. She looked around the library, taking in details she had missed in her exhaustion the night before. Shafts of early morning light cut through the dusty air, illuminating tiny particles that danced like fairy dust. The silence, which had seemed oppressive before, now felt almost reverent.

The two women settled at one of the library's grand old tables, the wood scarred with centuries of use but still sturdy. Jeanette couldn't help but wonder about the countless scholars who must have sat at this very table over the years long ago, poring over arcane texts and unravelling the mysteries of magic.

Between bites of a surprisingly delicious sandwich – filled with some kind of herb-infused cheese that seemed to invigorate her with each mouthful – Jeanette listened as Heidi explained her presence in the abandoned library.

"My parents are both respected witches,"

Heidi said, a note of pride mingling with something that sounded like anxiety. "They want me to follow in their footsteps, to be accepted into Arcanum Academy. It's... it's a lot of pressure. That's why I come here to study. The solitude helps me focus."

Jeanette couldn't help but notice the conflicting emotions that played across Heidi's face as she spoke. There was genuine passion when she discussed her studies, but also a palpable undercurrent of insecurity, as if she feared she might not measure up to the high expectations placed upon her.

"Arcanum Academy?" Jeanette repeated curiously. "I'm not familiar with it. What can you tell me about it?"

Heidi's eyes lit up at the question.

"Oh, it's the most prestigious school of magic in the entire region," she said excitedly. "Only the most talented and dedicated witches are accepted. The things they teach there... spells and rituals that most people can only dream of. My parents met there, actually. That's part of why they're so set on me going there. They see it as a family tradition."

Jeanette nodded, sensing the burden of family expectations that seemed to weigh on Heidi.

"And is that what you want?" she asked gently.

Heidi bit her lip, considering the question.

"I... I'm not sure," she admitted. "I love magic, I truly do. But sometimes I wonder if I'm pursuing it for myself or for my parents. And the entrance exams are notoriously difficult. What if I'm not good enough?"

"From what I've seen, you seem incredibly dedicated," Jeanette said kindly. "I'm sure you're more capable than you give yourself credit for."

"Thank you," said Heidi, giving Jeanette a grateful smile. "That means a lot... What about you? How did you come to be sleeping in an abandoned library?"

Jeanette took a deep breath, steeling herself to recount her ordeal. She told Heidi about the vampire who had cursed her hometown, about being unjustly accused and driven out by her own neighbours, about the panic she had felt as she'd fled from those she had once called friends.

"And then, just when I thought all hope was lost, I encountered a reaper," Jeanette said. "She brought me here."

"You need to be careful, Jeanette," said Heidi, her voice tinged with disbelief and worry. "Why would a reaper want to help you? They're not known for their benevolence towards witches. They're beings of death and endings. Did she ask anything of you?"

"Yes," Jeanette answered, seeing no reason to hide anything from Heidi. "She brought me here so I can learn the magic I need to save my town – to defeat the vampire who caused all this suffering. I couldn't turn that down, even if it means co-operating with a being I've been taught to distrust. I know it's risky, but with everything stacked against me, with nowhere to go, I had to take a leap of faith. And so, here I am."

Heidi opened her mouth as if to argue further, but Jeanette pressed on.

"Defeating that vampire and breaking the curse over Millbrook is all that matters to me. If helping a reaper is what it takes to achieve that, then so be it."

Chapter Six

As the afternoon sun cast long shadows through the library's dusty windows, Jeanette stirred from her makeshift bed. Her earlier conversation with Heidi had left her feeling both hopeful and overwhelmed, and the emotional toll of recounting her recent ordeal had driven her back to the comforting embrace of sleep. Now, as she blinked away the remnants of her slumber, she found herself once again in the cavernous silence of the abandoned library.

Sitting up slowly, her gaze fell upon Heidi, who was hunched over the same table where they had shared sandwiches earlier. The blonde witch was completely absorbed in a thick, leather-bound tome, her brow furrowed in concentration as her eyes darted across the pages. Not wanting to disturb Heidi's intense focus, Jeanette quietly rose to her feet, deciding to take this opportunity to properly explore.

As she padded softly between the towering shelves, Jeanette marvelled at the sheer volume of knowledge contained within these walls. The comforting scent of old parchment and leather bindings filled the air, speaking of ancient wisdom and forgotten lore. Her fingers trailed lightly over the spines of countless books, each one promising secrets and revelations.

The variety of subjects was staggering. Entire sections were devoted to different branches of magic – from elemental manipulation to potion brewing, from divination to transmutation. But it was the deeply paranormal subjects that truly caught Jeanette's attention. Her eyes widened as she discovered shelf after shelf dedicated to creatures of myth and legend, magical beasts, and supernatural phenomena.

With a sense of purpose, she roamed the aisles, selecting volumes that caught her eye until the stack threatened to topple. Then, finally, she began gathering the books she had noted earlier, feeling that they would be the most relevant to her dire situation. 'Compendium of Vampiric Weaknesses' was the first, its cover adorned with an intricate silver design that shimmered in the fading daylight. Next came 'Advanced Defensive Spellcraft', a weighty tome promising protection against dark forces. Finally, she added 'Curses and Their Countermeasures', hoping it might hold the key to breaking the malevolent influence over her hometown.

Arms laden with her chosen texts, Jeanette made her way back to the table where Heidi was sitting. Despite the abundance of empty tables throughout the vast library, Jeanette found herself drawn to the companionship offered by the other witch's presence. She settled into a chair opposite Heidi, careful not to disturb her new friend's concentration.

As Jeanette delved into her research, the magnitude of the task before her began to sink in. Page after page revealed spells and rituals of daunting complexity, far beyond anything she had encountered in her previous magical education. The sheer depth of knowledge required to combat a vampire was overwhelming, and she couldn't help but let out a heavy sigh.

The sound, soft though it was, broke through Heidi's intense focus. The blonde witch looked up, concern etched on her features as she took in Jeanette's troubled expression.

"What's wrong?" Heidi asked, her voice gentle and tinged with genuine worry.

Jeanette gestured helplessly at the open book before her.

"These spells... they're all new to me," she admitted, frustration evident in her tone. "I've always considered myself to be a competent witch, but this? This is far beyond anything I've ever attempted."

Intrigued, Heidi leaned across the table, her own studies momentarily forgotten. She tilted her head to get a better look at the spell book Jeanette had been poring over. As her eyes scanned the pages, a spark of recognition lit up her face.

"Oh, I know this one!" she exclaimed excitedly. "It's a complex spell, but I've studied it before. Here, let me show you."

With a grace born of countless hours of

practice, Heidi rose to her feet and took a few steps away from the table. She closed her eyes, took a deep breath, and began to murmur an incantation. Jeanette watched in awe as Heidi put her hands together; they began to shimmer, a warm orange light emanating from her palms.

Suddenly, with a soft whoosh, a ball of fire sprang to life between Heidi's hands. The flames danced and flickered, casting an amber glow across her face. What struck Jeanette most was the absolute control Heidi exhibited over the magical fire. There was no fear, no hesitation – just a serene confidence as she manipulated the flames, causing them to grow and shrink at will.

After a few moments of this impressive display, Heidi calmly closed her hands, extinguishing the fire as easily as blowing out a candle. She turned to Jeanette with a shy smile, as if suddenly self-conscious of her demonstration.

Jeanette sat in stunned silence for a moment before finding her voice.

"That was incredible, Heidi," she said,

genuine admiration colouring her words. "The level of control you have… it's amazing."

As the reality of what she had just witnessed sank in, Jeanette felt a mixture of emotions washing over her. On the one hand, she was in awe of Heidi's skill and grateful to be in the company of such talent. On the other, the demonstration had driven home just how much she would need to learn in order to stand a chance against a vampire.

"Heidi," Jeanette said sincerely, "you should have more confidence in yourself and your skills. Your dedication to studying magic has clearly taken you far beyond the capabilities of an average witch. What you just did… that's the kind of magic I need to master if I'm to have any hope of defeating the vampire and saving my town."

"Thank you," said Heidi, her voice soft but laced with gratitude as a blush crept across her cheeks. "That means a lot to me."

As the last rays of sunlight faded from the library windows, Heidi pulled an ornate pocket watch from her robes and glanced anxiously at the time.

"I didn't realise it had got so late," she exclaimed. "I'd better head back home; my parents will be expecting me."

Jeanette felt a pang of disappointment at the thought of Heidi leaving, but she nodded in understanding. Heidi began gathering her things, carefully placing her books and notes into a well-worn satchel.

As she prepared to leave, Heidi turned back to Jeanette with a warm smile.

"I'll be back tomorrow," she promised. "And I'll bring more food and drink for you. We can't have you studying on an empty stomach."

Jeanette felt a wave of gratitude wash over her. In this strange and uncertain time, Heidi's kindness was a beacon of hope.

Chapter Seven

The second day in the library dawned with a sense of purpose for Jeanette. As promised, Heidi had returned, bringing with her a basket filled with sandwiches and a flask of coffee. The aroma of freshly brewed coffee and herb-infused bread filled the air, momentarily chasing away the musty scent of ancient tomes that permeated the library.

After sharing their meal in a companionable silence, the two witches settled at a table into their respective studies. The soft rustle of turning pages and the occasional scratch of a quill on parchment were the only sounds that disturbed the library's tranquil atmosphere. Jeanette found herself immersed in the 'Compendium of Vampiric Weaknesses', her eyes eagerly scanning the yellowed pages for any information that might be of use.

As the hours passed, Jeanette's excitement grew. Her finger traced the lines of text, noting every detail, every nuance of vampiric lore. Suddenly, she stopped abruptly, her pulse quickening as her eyes fell on a passage that sent a thrill of urgency through her. There, laid out in meticulous detail, was a list of ingredients and instructions for a spell designed to weaken a vampire.

Jeanette's mind whirled with possibilities. This was exactly the kind of magic she had been searching for, a ray of hope in her seemingly insurmountable task. The spell promised to diminish a vampire's supernatural strength and speed, rendering the creature more vulnerable to attack. It was complex, certainly, but not beyond her capabilities, especially with the resources of this vast library at her disposal.

Unable to contain her excitement, Jeanette looked up from her book, her eyes sparkling with newfound determination.

"Heidi!" she exclaimed, her voice breaking the library's silence like a thunderclap. "I've found something incredible!"

Heidi looked up from her own studies, her brow furrowed in a mixture of concern and curiosity.

"What is it?" she asked, marking her place in her book with a slender ribbon.

"It's a spell to weaken vampires!" Jeanette declared, her words tumbling out in a rush as she leaned across the table, pushing the book towards Heidi and pointing to the passage. "This could be exactly what I need to defeat the creature that's cursed my hometown! Look at these ingredients – if I can find them, I might actually stand a chance!"

Heidi's eyes skimmed over the text, and for a moment, she seemed to share in Jeanette's enthusiasm. Her lips curved into a smile, and she nodded appreciatively at the complexity of the spell. However, as Jeanette continued to expound on her plans, a subtle shift came over Heidi's demeanour.

"We need to go to the nearest shop," Jeanette insisted, already half-rising from her chair. "If we can source these ingredients, I can start practicing the spell right away."

It was then that Jeanette noticed the change in Heidi's expression. The blonde witch's smile had faded to be replaced by a look of hesitation, perhaps even worry.

"What's wrong?" Jeanette asked. "Don't you think this is great?"

Heidi's eyes darted away, avoiding Jeanette's questioning gaze.

"I'm not sure," she said. "Maybe we should think about this more carefully."

Jeanette couldn't understand the sudden shift in Heidi's attitude. Just moments ago, they had been sharing in the excitement of discovery. Now, Heidi seemed almost reluctant to engage with the idea.

Before Jeanette could press further, Heidi abruptly stood up.

"I've just remembered," she said, her words coming out in a rush, "there's a set of books I need to consult. On a different shelf. I'll... I'll be right back."

Without waiting for a response, Heidi

hurried away, disappearing behind a row of towering bookshelves.

Jeanette sat there, stunned by the sudden turn of events. Her perceptive nature, honed by years of observing the subtle energies of magic, told her that there was more to Heidi's behaviour than a simple need for different books. Something was amiss, and she was determined to find out what it was.

After giving Heidi a few moments, Jeanette rose from her chair and headed in the same direction. She found Heidi in a secluded corner of the library, pretending to peruse a shelf, but clearly lost in thought.

"Heidi," Jeanette said softly, causing the other witch to jump slightly. "Please, tell me what's going on. Why are you suddenly so reluctant about this spell? I thought you'd be happy for me."

Heidi turned to face Jeanette, conflict evident in her eyes. She opened her mouth as if to speak, then closed it again, shaking her head.

"Come on, Heidi," said Jeanette, her voice taking on a pleading tone. "Let's get some fresh air. We can walk to the shop together, talk things over. It'll do us both good to get out of this library for a bit, don't you think?"

Heidi looked away, her gaze distant as though she was wrestling with some internal struggle. Finally, after a long pause, she sighed and met Jeanette's gaze.

"Jeanette," she said, her voice heavy with resignation, "there is no shop."

"What do you mean, there's no shop?" Jeanette asked in confusion. "Surely there must be a town nearby, or..."

Heidi glanced around nervously, as if afraid they might be overheard, despite them being the only two in the vast library.

"Jeanette," she said, her voice steady but tinged with sadness, "you're not... we're not in your world anymore. You're not in the abandoned library the reaper wanted to take you to. You're in a completely different realm."

The words hit Jeanette like a physical blow. She staggered back, her mind reeling as she tried to process this revelation.

"A different realm?" she repeated, her voice faint with disbelief. "But... but that's impossible. I've seen the outside of the library. I..."

"I wasn't going to tell you," Heidi admitted, her expression softening with sympathy, "but you've been so kind to me. You deserve to know the truth, especially since you've already started questioning whether you can leave the library."

Jeanette shook her head, struggling to make sense of it all.

"But I've seen the outside," she insisted again, clinging to this one piece of what felt like undeniable truth.

"Yes," Heidi acknowledged gently, "you've seen the immediate surroundings. But have you ventured beyond that?"

The realisation that Heidi could be right – that she hadn't actually explored beyond the library grounds – hit Jeanette hard. She felt her legs weaken beneath her, and she leaned against a bookshelf for support. Seeing Jeanette's distress, Heidi stepped forward, placing a comforting hand on her arm.

"Come with me," Heidi said softly. "I'll show you."

With gentle guidance, Heidi led Jeanette through the library's grand doors and out into the open air. At first, everything seemed normal – the overgrown grounds, the dilapidated fence in the immediate distance. As they walked a little further though, beyond the boundaries Jeanette had subconsciously accepted, her world tilted on its axis.

Where there should have been a road, or fields, or any sign of civilisation, there was instead a shimmering, ethereal barrier. Walls of swirling bright colours danced before her eyes, creating a mesmerising yet terrifying boundary. The barrier pulsed with an inner light, its surface constantly shifting and changing like a soap bubble caught in the sunlight.

Jeanette took a hesitant step forward, her hand outstretched as if to touch the impossible spectacle before her. As she drew closer, she could make out individual hues within the swirling mass – deep sapphire blues that reminded her of the night sky, vibrant emerald greens like the heart of an ancient forest, fiery reds and oranges that seemed to flicker and dance like living flames. These colours bled into one another, creating new shades and patterns with each passing moment.

The barrier wasn't just visual; Jeanette could feel it. An electric tingle ran across her skin, raising goosebumps along her arms. The air near the boundary felt charged, as if a lightning storm was perpetually on the verge of breaking. She could hear it too – a faint, melodic hum that seemed to resonate deep within her bones, a sound that was both beautiful and slightly unnerving.

As she stood there, transfixed by the spectacle, Jeanette's mind raced to make sense of what she was seeing. This barrier, this impossible wall of light and colour, made it abundantly clear that within this realm, there was nowhere else to go beyond the abandoned library and its immediate grounds.

She stood rooted to the spot, her eyes wide with shock and disbelief. The familiar world she had known all her life was gone and had been replaced by this bizarre, confined space that defied all logic.

"What is this place?" she asked, her voice trembling as she turned to face Heidi. "How is this possible?"

"It's a realm beyond your own," Heidi explained gently, her face a mask of sympathy and understanding. "A place where the rules of your world don't apply. Your mind intervened and brought you here, Jeanette – to this pocket of existence separate from everything you've ever known."

As the enormity of her situation began to sink in, a wave of dizziness swept over Jeanette. The implications were staggering. The vampire she had sworn to defeat seemed impossibly far away now, separated not only by distance, but by the very fabric of reality.

"I'm so sorry, Jeanette," Heidi said softly. "I know this must be overwhelming for you, but you're not alone here. I promise you that."

Chapter Eight

The swirling, ethereal barrier that defined the boundaries of this impossible realm seemed to close in around Jeanette, overwhelming her with the shock of her new reality. Unable to bear it any longer, she turned around and fled, her feet carrying her swiftly back towards the abandoned library.

She burst through the heavy wooden doors, the familiar musty scent of old books doing little to calm her frayed nerves. She stumbled between the towering shelves, her vision blurred by unshed tears, until she found herself at one of the library's many tables. With a choked sob, she collapsed into a chair, burying her face in her hands as the full impact of her situation washed over her.

Time seemed to slow as she sat there, lost in the tumult of her own thoughts. But gradually, she became aware of a gentle presence beside her. She looked up to see Heidi standing there, her expression one of concern and compassion.

"I'm so sorry," Heidi said softly, pulling up a chair and sitting close to Jeanette. "I know this is a lot to take in."

Jeanette tried to speak, but found her voice choked with emotion. Heidi reached out, placing a comforting hand on her arm. The touch, warm and reassuring, helped to anchor Jeanette, giving her something tangible to focus on.

"Jeanette," Heidi said firmly, "there's something you need to understand about all of this – about where you are, and why you're here."

Jeanette looked up, her eyes red-rimmed but attentive. Heidi took a deep breath before continuing.

"This realm, this library... it's all in your mind. Your subconscious created it as a defence mechanism."

Jeanette blinked, struggling to comprehend.

"In my mind? But... how? Why?"

"Deep down, you know that reapers aren't to be trusted," Heidi said, her expression turning grave. "When the reaper began to transport you to their chosen destination, to the abandoned library that they had in mind, your mind intervened. It brought you here instead, to this mental construct, as a way of protecting you."

Fragments of memory began to surface in Jeanette's thoughts. The reaper's cold touch, the sensation of being pulled through space and time, and then... a moment of resistance, of fear. Had that been her mind asserting control?

"But why?" Jeanette asked. "Why would my mind do this?"

"Because deep down, you know the truth about the reaper's intentions," said Heidi, leaning in closer. "The reaper wants you to defeat the vampire who has cursed your hometown, yes, but not for altruistic reasons. Once the vampire is out of her way, the reaper plans to take over."

A chill ran down Jeanette's spine as the implications of Heidi's words sank in.

"And what about me?" she asked, dreading the answer.

"The reaper would kill you, Jeanette. Why would a being like that want a powerful witch standing in her way?"

The pieces began to fall into place in Jeanette's mind, a terrible picture forming from the scattered fragments of her memories and fears.

"So when the vampire came to my town and started the curse..."

"The reaper saw an opportunity," Heidi finished. "A chance to use you to eliminate a powerful rival."

Jeanette felt sick to her stomach. She had been so focused on wanting to save Millbrook, on the burning desire to prove her innocence, that she had never stopped to question the reaper's motives. How could she have been so blind?

"What should I do?" Jeanette asked, her voice trembling with a mixture of dread and anger.

Heidi gave her a sad smile.

"Remember, Jeanette, I'm just a part of this realm your mind has created. I can offer advice, but ultimately, the decision is yours."

"Please," said Jeanette, mindful of the strange logic of the situation, "tell me what you think I should do."

"It would be unwise to do the reaper's bidding," Heidi said firmly. "Killing the vampire would only play into her plans."

"Then what should I do?" Jeanette asked, frustrated.

"Maybe," Heidi said slowly, a spark of inspiration seeming to light in her eyes, "you need to use your magic in a different way. Instead of confronting either the vampire or the reaper directly, what if you could create a magical intervention that would force them to fight each other?"

"A spell to pit them against each other?" said

Jeanette, her eyes widening as she considered the possibility. "To make them fight to the death?"

"Exactly!" said Heidi, excitement growing in her voice. "Think about it, Jeanette. If you could engineer a situation where the vampire and the reaper had to battle each other, you wouldn't have to face either of them directly."

As the idea took root in her mind, Jeanette felt a surge of hope for the first time since learning the full extent of her predicament.

"And if they destroyed each other..."

"It would solve everyone's problems," Heidi finished. "Your town would be free of the vampire's curse, and the reaper's plans would be thwarted. You and the people of Millbrook would be safe."

Jeanette sat back in her chair, her mind whirling with the possibilities this new plan presented. It was audacious, certainly, and would require magic far beyond anything she had attempted before. But it also offered a way out of the seemingly impossible situation she was in.

"You're brilliant," Jeanette said, a note of determination creeping into her voice. "This could actually work."

Heidi beamed at her, clearly pleased to have been of help.

"Remember though," she said gently, "I'm just a manifestation of your mind. This idea, this solution – it came from you. You have the strength and the wisdom within you to overcome this challenge."

With a renewed sense of purpose, Jeanette stood up, her eyes scanning the towering bookshelves around her.

"Well then," she said, a hint of her old confidence returning, "I suppose we have some studying to do."

"Indeed," said Heidi as she rose from her seat, her expression warm and encouraging.

As they set off into the depths of the library, Jeanette felt a complex blend of emotions swirling within her. Fear and uncertainty were still present, but they were now tempered by a greater sense of focus and a spark of hope. As she began to pull volumes from the shelves, she silently vowed to make the most of this strange twist of fate. She would learn, she would grow, and when the time came, she would be ready to turn the vampire and reaper against each other, using their own dark ambitions to her advantage.

Chapter Nine

As the first light of dawn crept through the dusty windows of the abandoned library, Jeanette found herself once again seated at the now-familiar table, a spread of sandwiches and coffee before her. Heidi, true to her word, had once again arrived with provisions, her gentle smile a comforting constant in this strange realm.

The previous afternoon had been a whirlwind of research and study. Together, they had scoured the library's vast collection, poring over ancient tomes and arcane scrolls in search of a spell that could manipulate both vampire and reaper. Now, as the morning wore on, Jeanette found herself lost in the pages of a particularly deep treatise on manipulative magic. The words swam before her eyes, each sentence a puzzle to be unravelled. She was so engrossed, so focused.

"Jeanette!" Heidi suddenly exclaimed, her excitement impossible to ignore. "I think I've found it!"

Jeanette's head snapped up, her heart racing with anticipation.

"That's fantastic," she said. "What is it?"

But as Heidi proceeded to explain, Jeanette felt a strange sensation beginning to wash over her. The world around her started to blur, the edges of reality softening and distorting. Heidi's voice, once clear and close, now seemed to come from a great distance, echoing strangely in her ears.

"The spell requires... you'll need to... focus on..." Heidi's words faded in and out, crucial information lost in the growing haze.

Panic gripped Jeanette as she realised what was happening. The realm she had come to know, this sanctuary of knowledge with Heidi by her side, was slipping away. The abandoned library, the books, even Heidi herself began to fade like mist.

With a jolt, Jeanette found herself blinking awake, the cold, damp grass of the familiar graveyard pressing against her legs. The stark reality of her situation came crashing back – she was no longer in the comforting confines of the abandoned library, but back in the world where she was a fugitive, chased from her home and tasked with an impossible mission by a duplicitous reaper.

Jeanette scrambled to her feet. The graveyard stretched out around her, silent and foreboding even in the daylight. Tombstones cast long shadows across the overgrown weeds, and a chilling wind whipped through the trees, carrying with it the scent of decay and forgotten memories.

"No, no, no," Jeanette muttered, her voice hoarse with desperation. "I can't be back here. Not now. Not when I was so close to the answer!"

She began to pace frantically among the graves. How could she get back to the other realm, to Heidi and the vital information she held? Jeanette wracked her brain, trying to recall any spell, any incantation that might bridge the gap between the two worlds.

As she wandered, her fingers trailed over cold stone markers, her eyes unseeing as she delved deep into her magical knowledge. Perhaps a trance state? A potion to induce visions? But no, she had no ingredients here, no tools at her disposal.

Just as despair threatened to overwhelm her, Jeanette felt a wave of dizziness wash over her. The world tilted on its axis, and she found herself falling, consciousness slipping away like water through her fingers.

When she opened her eyes again, Jeanette found herself back at the library table, Heidi's concerned face swimming into focus before her.

"Jeanette! Are you alright?" Heidi asked worriedly. "You seemed to... fade away for a moment there."

Jeanette blinked, relief flooding through her.

"Heidi! Oh, thank goodness. I was back in the graveyard – in the real world. I thought I'd lost you – lost all of this – forever."

"It's alright," Heidi said. "You're back now. But this realm... it's not stable. It's a creation of your mind, remember? Evidently, it's being pulled in different directions."

"It's horrible – the uncertainty of it all. One moment I'm here, with you, on the verge of finding the answers I need. The next, I'm alone in a cold graveyard, with no idea of what to do."

It then dawned on Jeanette just how much Heidi's presence had come to mean to her. In this strange, mental construct, Heidi had become more than just a figment of her imagination – she was a friend, a confidante, a beacon of hope in the darkness of this predicament.

"I'll miss you so much," Jeanette said, her voice thick with emotion. "If it comes to pass that I can no longer return to this realm, I want you to know that you've been such a comfort, such a help. I don't know how I would have managed without you."

"I'll miss you too," Heidi said sincerely, "but let's not worry about that now. We have more pressing matters to attend to – namely, the spell that could save your life and your town."

"You're right. Of course," said Jeanette, nodding and forcing herself to focus on the task at hand. "You said you'd found something?"

"Yes," Heidi replied, her excitement returning as she pulled a large leather-bound tome closer, its pages yellowed with age. "It's a complex spell, but I believe it's exactly what we need. It's called 'The Puppeteer's Gambit'."

"Tell me everything," Jeanette insisted, leaning in to scan the intricate diagrams and abundant text.

"Ok," said Heidi, her voice steady and clear. "The spell works by creating magical tethers between two targets – in this case, the vampire and the reaper. These tethers act as conduits for emotions and impulses – specifically anger, aggression, and the desire for confrontation."

"But how can I cast it remotely?" Jeanette asked, keenly aware of her inability to summon the reaper at will.

"That's the brilliant part," Heidi replied. "The spell doesn't require your physical presence. It works through sympathetic magic. You'll need personal items from both the vampire and the reaper – possessions they've handled recently. With these items, you can create magical proxies and cast the spell from a safe distance."

"In one cast?"

"Yes. The spell will gradually intensify feelings of hostility and paranoia between the vampire and the reaper. It will plant suggestions in their minds and make them see each other as threats that must be eliminated. Eventually, they'll be compelled to confront one another."

"And then they'll fight to the death?" Jeanette asked, in both awe and trepidation.

"If all goes according to plan, yes. They'll destroy each other."

As Jeanette absorbed the details of the spell, she felt a glimmer of hope spark within her. It was dangerous, certainly, and would require all of her effort and concentration, but it offered a way out of her seemingly impossible situation – a chance to save Millbrook without having to directly confront either the vampire or the reaper.

"This could work," she said, alight with determination. "It's risky, but it's the best chance we have."

"I believe in you," said Heidi, pride evident in her expression. "You have the strength and the skill to make this work."

They bent their heads together over the spell book, delving into the intricacies of The Puppeteer's Gambit. In the back of her mind, Jeanette knew that her time in this realm might be limited, that at any moment she could find herself back in the cold, hard reality of the graveyard. But for now, she pushed those fears aside, focusing all of her energy on memorising every detail of the spell that could be her salvation.

Chapter Ten

Jeanette leaned back in her chair, struggling to push aside the worry that lingered in her mind. The Puppeteer's Gambit spell offered a glimmer of hope, but the practicalities of obtaining the necessary components seemed daunting.

"This spell... it's brilliant, truly," she said to Heidi, "but how are we supposed to get personal items from both the vampire and the reaper? I can't exactly walk up to either of them and ask them to make a donation."

"Think, Jeanette," Heidi said firmly. "Think hard and deep. There must be a way."

The two witches fell into a contemplative silence, the only sound the soft rustling of ancient pages and the occasional creak of the library's timeworn structure. Suddenly, Jeanette's eyes widened with realisation.

"The reaper!" she exclaimed. "When we met in the graveyard, her hair was long and flowing in the wind. It's possible... no, likely, that a strand or two might have come loose."

"Yes!" said Heidi, nodding enthusiastically. "And the reaper's hair – you said it was a distinctive midnight black, didn't you? In a place as rarely visited as that graveyard, strands like that would surely be unmistakeable."

Jeanette felt a surge of hope, but it was quickly tempered by the reality of their other target.

"But the vampire... that's a different story altogether," she said. "I can't go back to Millbrook, not with everyone believing I'm responsible for the curse."

"Perhaps we need to think outside the box," said Heidi, her brow furrowing in concentration. "Is there anywhere just on the outskirts of town where the vampire might have been recently?"

"Hmm..." Jeanette mused. "Even if there was, how would we know what possessions the vampire might have dropped, if any?"

"What if we could use magic to acquire something from the vampire, make it materialise right here in the library?" Heidi offered, a spark of inspiration in her eyes.

"A summoning spell? But they are incredibly complex, especially over such a distance."

"Complex, yes," Heidi agreed, "but not impossible."

As the implications of Heidi's suggestion sank in, Jeanette's mind raced with possibilities.

"Wait a moment," she said thoughtfully. "If we're considering using magic to acquire something from the vampire... couldn't we do the same for the reaper? It would save me the risk of having to return to the graveyard. I can't bear the thought of not being able to get back to this realm, not now."

Heidi's face lit up with a brilliant smile.

"Jeanette, that's perfect! Yes, we could absolutely use the same method for both. Yes, it will take some work, but it's safer, more reliable, and we can do it all from right here in the library."

With their new plan in place, the two witches set to work, scouring the library's vast collection for the perfect summoning spell. As they searched, Jeanette couldn't help but marvel at Heidi's quick thinking and magical knowledge.

"You know, Heidi," Jeanette said, pausing in her search to look at her friend, "you really are a brilliant witch. You should have more confidence in your abilities. That academy you mentioned before? They'd be lucky to have you."

The compliment caused a faint blush to rise in Heidi's cheeks.

"Thank you," she said. "I appreciate it very much."

Hours passed as they pored over ancient tomes and scrolls, searching for the perfect spell. Finally, with a triumphant cry, Heidi held up a weathered grimoire.

"Here! The Ethereal Acquisition Ritual. It's perfect for what we need."

Jeanette and Heidi hunched over the grimoire. The yellowed pages were covered in intricate diagrams and densely packed with complex incantations, their margins filled with warnings and notations in a long-forgotten script. This spell was not just challenging; it was steeped in dark and taboo magic, the kind whispered about in fearful tones by even the most seasoned witches. A mistake could have catastrophic consequences.

"It won't be simple," said Jeanette. "I wish we didn't have to do this at all. There's so much that could go wrong."

"I agree," said Heidi. "We can't afford even the smallest margin of error. Just hold on to how great it will be if we can get it to work."

"Are you ready?" Jeanette uttered cautiously.

Heidi nodded, her hand trembling slightly as she reached into her bag, pulling out crushed herbs and powdered gemstones – essential components in any witch's basic kit.

"We can do this," she murmured, more to herself than to Jeanette.

They began with the reaper's ritual. Heidi's hands moved with practiced precision, drawing a complex series of magical circles on the cold, dusty floor. Each stroke of her hand was deliberate, the herbs and gemstones leaving a shimmering trail. Jeanette's heart pounded in her chest as she watched, her own fingers tingling in expectation of the spell's power.

"Candles," Heidi said, her voice steady despite the tension in the air.

Jeanette diligently positioned the candles they had gathered from various corners of the library, arranging them at key points around the perimeter. Once everything was in place, Heidi took out a small box of matches from her pocket and struck one, lighting each candle in turn. Their flames flickered wildly, as if in anticipation of the potent magic about to be unleashed.

Jeanette took her place opposite Heidi, and for a brief, silent moment, they locked eyes – a shared, unspoken agreement passing between them. With a steady breath, they began the chant, their voices merging in perfect harmony. The air grew thick, heavy with the intensity of their combined power. The energy was palpable, a living thing that coiled around them as their voices rose and fell. Jeanette could feel the magic thrumming beneath her skin, a heady mix of electricity and exhilaration. The room seemed to close in on them, the shadows deepening as their chant reached a fevered pitch.

With a sudden, blinding flash of midnight-blue light, a single strand of jet-black hair materialised in the centre of the circle. Jeanette was in awe.

"We did it," she said breathily, a grin spreading across her face.

"One down," Heidi said, her voice barely concealing her excitement as her eyes sparkled with triumph. "Ready for the next one?"

Jeanette nodded, her focus sharpening as she readied herself.

The vampire's ritual was even more daunting. The air seemed to crackle with dark energy, the resistance pressing down on them like a physical weight. Jeanette's hands shook as she mirrored Heidi's movements, the two of them working in synchronisation. Every breath felt like a battle, every word of the incantation a struggle against the encroaching darkness.

"Keep going," Heidi urged, her voice strained but determined. "We can do this."

Jeanette's throat burned with the effort of chanting, her vision blurring as the magic surged around them. She could see the fatigue on Heidi's face. They were pushing themselves to the limit, their voices hoarse and raw with exertion.

Just when it seemed the spell might falter, a sudden burst of crimson light bathed the room, so bright that Jeanette had to squint against its intensity. As the otherworldly glow began to fade, she felt a rush of relief as she spotted the small, ornate silver ring before them, its surface gleaming ominously. She and Heidi collapsed to their knees, exhausted.

"We did it," Heidi said, reaching out and brushing her fingers against the ring. "It's real."

Jeanette picked up the reaper's hair, its

peculiar shimmer sending a shiver down her spine.

"And so is this," she replied, her voice hushed with fascination.

The library's shadows flickered and danced as Jeanette and Heidi stood amidst the lingering magic, the air humming with the energy of their successful rituals. Every breath felt charged, and even the creaking of the old building seemed to vibrate with new, potent life. They exchanged a look, the joy of their accomplishment slowly settling into the realisation that the possessions they had summoned would need to be stored somewhere safe.

"Where should we put them?" Jeanette asked, her voice low and thoughtful, her eyes scanning the room with a newfound wariness.

Heidi pursed her lips, considering the options.

"At the far end of the library," she said, "where they can't be accidentally triggered by any other magic we'll be working on."

They moved through the dim aisles. It was Heidi who spotted it first: a small, elaborate wooden box tucked away on a high shelf, almost hidden by shadows and layers of dust that had settled over the years.

"Look at this," she said, reaching up to carefully pull the box down.

"It's perfect," Jeanette murmured, running her fingers over the intricately carved design on the lid and appreciating the smoothly polished dark wood on the sides.

They opened the box, the hinges creaking softly. Inside, the lining was a rich deep-red velvet, its plush surface catching the light in a way that made it appear almost iridescent. Gently, they placed the reaper's hair and the vampire's ring inside, the items resting carefully within the material's embrace.

"We should put this somewhere out of the way," Heidi suggested, closing the lid with a soft click. "We need to be sure that the ambient magical energy from our other spellwork won't interfere with it."

Jeanette nodded in agreement, her eyes scanning the area once more.

"How about up there?" she said, pointing to a dusty alcove high above the library's main floor.

Heidi looked up, a slow smile spreading across her face.

"Perfect," she said. "Let's put it there."

With a bit of effort, Jeanette scaled the towering shelves, her hands finding purchase on the weathered wood as she climbed higher. The shelves groaned under her weight, and dust swirled in the stale air around her. Finally, she reached the alcove and carefully placed the box, ensuring it was secure but would still be accessible when needed.

Upon her descent, Jeanette felt relieved, knowing their hard-won items were safely stored, hidden among the vast, silent rows of forgotten knowledge. As they moved farther from the box's location and back to their table, her mind began to churn with thoughts of the next spell they needed to master: The Puppeteer's Gambit.

Chapter Eleven

Jeanette's heart raced as she stood in the centre of the abandoned library, her eyes fixed on the intricate chalk symbols etched across the worn wooden floor. The air around her crackled with the anticipation of what she and Heidi were about to attempt. Days of rigorous study had led to this moment, every waking hour devoted to mastering the complex intricacies of the Puppeteer's Gambit spell.

As she took a deep breath to steady her nerves, Jeanette couldn't help but reflect on the enormity of the situation. Since her exile from Millbrook, each day must have been a nightmare for the townspeople under the vampire's reign of terror. Though they had wrongly accused her of being behind the curse, she couldn't shake the images of her neighbours' faces, twisted with fear. The thought of their ongoing misery gnawed at her conscience, strengthening her resolve to see this through.

"Are you ready?" Heidi asked, her soft voice breaking through Jeanette's reverie.

"As ready as we'll ever be," Jeanette replied, managing a small smile. "Let's go over it one more time, just to be sure."

Together, they meticulously reviewed each step of the spell. The fear of potential failure hung heavy in the air – a single oversight, no matter how minor, could unleash chaos beyond their control. Yet, with each step, Jeanette felt her confidence growing.

Once they were satisfied that every detail was committed to memory, Jeanette nodded to Heidi.

"It's time," she said. "Let's get the items."

They approached the end of the library where they had placed the box in the high alcove. Jeanette took the lead. She gripped the edges of the shelves, testing her footing on each one. Slowly, she climbed, dust swirling around her in the faint light.

Carefully, she lifted the box from the alcove and climbed back down, handing it to Heidi right away. With a shared sense of duty driving them onward, they returned to the centre of the library. Heidi gently placed the box on the table, and Jeanette opened it. Inside, just as they had left them, lay the reaper's single strand of midnight-black hair and the vampire's silver ring.

"I'm still amazed that we managed to get hold of them," Heidi said quietly, her voice tinged with awe.

Jeanette nodded in agreement. These seemingly insignificant items were the key they needed to change everything – to potentially free her hometown and clear her name. She lifted them from the box with reverent care, placing them at precise points within the chalk on the floor.

"This is it," she said, straightening up and meeting Heidi's gaze.

With a shared nod of understanding, they took their positions on opposite sides of the circle. Jeanette closed her eyes, taking a moment to centre herself and gather her magical energy. When she opened them, she saw Heidi doing the same, a faint aura of power beginning to shimmer around her.

"On three," Jeanette said softly. "One... two... three."

Their voices rose in unison, the ancient words of the Puppeteer's Gambit spell flowing from their lips with memorised precision. As they chanted, the air in the library began to thicken, swirling with currents of magical energy. The chalk lines of the diagram started to glow, softly at first, then with increasing intensity.

Jeanette felt the spell taking hold, invisible tendrils of magic reaching out from the circle. In her mind's eye, she could almost see the ethereal tethers forming – one connecting to the vampire, and the other to the reaper. These magical bonds would serve as conduits, channels through which she and Heidi could manipulate the emotions and impulses of their targets.

As the incantation reached its crescendo, Jeanette's skin tingled with the raw power coursing through her. The strand of hair and the ring began to levitate in the centre of the chalk circle, spinning slowly in midair as they pulsed with an almost-blinding light. With a final, forceful word, Jeanette and Heidi completed the spell, and a surge of magical energy erupted into the air, dissipating in a loud, ominous rumble.

As the glowing lines faded, the floating objects gently settled back to the floor. For a moment, all was still and silent in the library. Jeanette and Heidi exchanged a look, both breathing heavily from the exertion of the complex spell.

"Did it... did it work?" Jeanette asked hesitantly.

"I'm certain of it," said Heidi. "I could feel the connections forming. Now, we wait."

Jeanette sank to the floor, suddenly feeling drained. Heidi joined her. As they sat side by side in the silence, the magnitude of what they had just set in motion began to settle over them.

"How long do you think it will take?" Jeanette asked.

"I'm not sure," said Heidi. "The spell will work gradually, building up the hostility and paranoia between the vampire and the reaper. It could be days, maybe even weeks, before they're compelled to confront each other."

"And we just... wait here?"

"For now, yes," Heidi replied, reaching out to squeeze Jeanette's hand reassuringly. "We've done all we can. The spell will do its work, planting suggestions in their minds, making them see each other as threats that must be eliminated. Eventually, they'll have no choice but to face off against one another."

As the adrenaline of the moment began to fade, Jeanette found herself overcome with a mixture of emotions: hope for her hometown's liberation, fear of what might happen if the spell went awry, and a deep gratitude for Heidi's unwavering support through it all.

Chapter Twelve

Days had passed since Jeanette and Heidi had cast the Puppeteer's Gambit spell, each hour stretching into an eternity of anxious anticipation. They found solace in the familiar rhythms of study, with Jeanette taking on the role of tutor, testing Heidi's growing magical knowledge. As they sat at their table among the towering shelves of the abandoned library, Jeanette couldn't help but marvel at the transformation she had witnessed in her friend.

"You've come so far," she remarked, a note of pride in her voice. "When I first arrived here, you were so uncertain of your abilities. Now look at you – confidently reciting complex incantations and discussing advanced magical theory."

"I couldn't have done it without you," said Heidi, a shy smile playing across her lips. "Your encouragement means a lot to me."

Jeanette leaned back in her chair as she listened to Heidi's animated description of the prestigious academy she hoped to attend. The change in Heidi over their time together was remarkable, and Jeanette couldn't deny her swell of affection for the witch who had become her closest confidante in this strange, liminal space.

"I can just imagine you there," Jeanette said encouragingly. "Striding through those hallowed halls, your robes billowing behind you as you rush to your advanced transmutation class."

"You make it sound so glamorous," Heidi said with a chuckle. "I'll probably be tripping over my own feet and dropping scrolls everywhere."

"Nonsense," Jeanette replied. "You've grown so much, Heidi. Your confidence, your skill – you're going to take that academy by storm."

As Heidi opened her mouth to respond, she

stopped suddenly, a look of confusion passing over her face. Jeanette felt it too: a subtle shift in the air around them, as if the very atmosphere had become charged with an unseen energy. The change was so slight at first that she almost dismissed it as her imagination, a product of their days of anxious waiting.

But then it intensified.

What had started as a barely perceptible tremor quickly grew into a vibration that seemed to resonate through Jeanette's very bones. She anxiously gripped the sides of her chair, her knuckles whitening as the sensation grew stronger. It was as if every fibre of her being was attuned to a magical frequency or force beyond her control. The magic that usually lay dormant in her veins surged to life, responding to the pulsing energy that filled the room.

Books began to rattle on their shelves, some toppling to the floor with muffled thuds. The very floorboards beneath their feet seemed to quiver, as if the library itself was coming alive around them. When Jeanette's gaze locked with Heidi's, she saw her own mixture of shock and trepidation mirrored in her friend's eyes.

"Heidi," she said urgently, her voice barely audible above the low rumbling sound that now filled the air. "Can you feel that?"

Heidi nodded, her face pale but her eyes alight with a fierce intensity.

"It's like nothing I've ever experienced before," she said, her voice trembling as she grabbed the table. "The magical energy: it's overwhelming."

As the vibrations reached a fever pitch, Jeanette felt a surge of realisation washing over her. This wasn't just some random magical occurrence. No, this was something far more specific, something tied directly to the spell they had cast days ago.

"The Puppeteer's Gambit," she uttered, awe and a touch of fear colouring her tone. "Heidi, I think... I think it's working. The vampire and the reaper... they must be about to face off."

For a brief, shining moment, Jeanette revelled in the success of their audacious plan, her heart soaring with the knowledge that The Puppeteer's Gambit was working beyond their wildest expectations. But even as that elation coursed through her, an upsetting, harsh truth began to seep in, dousing the warmth of victory with the icy fingers of realisation.

Her euphoria crumbled to be replaced by a leaden weight that settled in the pit of her stomach. The magical tremors still pulsed around them, a constant reminder of the momentous events unfolding beyond the confines of this otherworldly library. She turned to Heidi with a mixture of determination and despair.

"I have to go," she said, her voice cracking under the strain of emotion, the words feeling like shards of glass in her throat, cutting and painful. "I need to leave this realm and witness the fight for myself."

The pronouncement hung in the air between them, loaded with implication. Jeanette watched as understanding dawned on Heidi's face, her expression shifting from confusion to comprehension, and finally, settling into a look of resigned sorrow.

"I agree that you need to see the fight with your own eyes," said Heidi, her effort at stoicism evident. "You need to witness the outcome, to know it's safe to return home for good."

Tears welled up in Jeanette's eyes, blurring her vision as the enormity of the situation hit her with brutal force. She reached out, grasping Heidi's hands in her own, clinging to her friend as if she could somehow anchor herself to this realm through sheer force of will.

"What if this is the end for us?" Jeanette asked, her voice trembling. "You've become so important to me, Heidi. I can't bear the thought of never seeing you again."

Jeanette's grip tightened on Heidi's hands, her fingers intertwining with her friend's as if trying to memorise the feeling, to hold on to this connection for as long as possible. The thought of leaving this place, of potentially never again seeing the person who had become her rock, her confidante, her partner in this extraordinary journey, was almost too much.

Heidi's eyes glistened with unshed tears, a mirror to Jeanette's anguish. But even in this moment of shared grief, she displayed the strength to be the pillar they both needed. She squared her shoulders and took a deep, steadying breath that seemed to fortify her resolve.

"Come on," she said, standing up and motioning for Jeanette to do the same. "You've got to leave now. Follow me."

With gentle but insistent pressure, Heidi's hand remained firmly wrapped around Jeanette's, guiding her towards the library's exit. With each step, Jeanette resisted a little, even though she understood the necessity of what had to be done.

"There's no time to lose," Heidi asserted, her voice wavering slightly despite her best efforts to remain strong. "Remember everything we've been through, everything we've learned."

Jeanette began to move with more certainty, propelled by Heidi's encouragement and the inexorable pull of destiny.

"Go," Heidi urged, compassionately but with unspoken pain.

Despite her anguish, Jeanette stole one last look at Heidi before tearing herself away. She broke into a run, her footsteps echoing through the vast library as she sprinted towards the exit. With each stride, she moved further from her friend, from the place they had shared, and into an uncertain future.

She burst through the library doors, barely registering the cold outdoor air as she ran towards the ethereal barrier marking the edge of this otherworldly realm. It shimmered and undulated, a gossamer-thin veil that now seemed as impenetrable as a fortress wall. She pushed against it, her mind straining with the effort to will herself back to reality.

The world around her began to warp and twist. Colours bled into one another, creating a dizzying kaleidoscope. Sounds distorted, stretching and compressing in ways that defied comprehension. For a terrifying moment, Jeanette feared she might be torn apart by the conflicting forces, her very essence splitting across the boundaries of multiple realms.

Just when she thought she could endure no more, when the strain of transition seemed poised to shatter her, everything snapped into focus. With a gasp that felt like her first breath after nearly drowning, Jeanette found herself lying on the damp grass of the graveyard. The real world solidified around her, familiar yet somehow uncomfortable after her time in the otherworldly library.

The magical tremors that had heralded this moment were far from subsiding. If anything, they pulsed through the earth with renewed intensity, vibrating through Jeanette's body with force. She scrambled to her feet, her legs unsteady as she tried to orientate herself in this suddenly vivid reality.

Pacing a little, still catching her breath and trying to process the abrupt transition, she became aware of something peculiar. The vibrations, already intense, seemed to grow even stronger when she moved in a particular direction. It was as if they were guiding her, pulling her towards something of immense magical significance.

With a start, Jeanette realised the tremors were leading her in the direction of Millbrook. The town was calling to her with an urgency she couldn't ignore.

She raced along the path, following the trail of magical energy that grew more potent with each step. As she crested the final hill and Millbrook came into view, she stumbled to a halt, horrified at the sight before her.

Chapter Thirteen

The familiar streets Jeanette had known since childhood were now twisted into a grotesque parody of their former selves, as if the very essence of the town had been corrupted by malevolence.

Buildings that had once stood proud and sturdy now sagged and warped, their structures seeming to melt under an invisible, infernal heat. Thatched roofs, once neatly trimmed and picturesque, now lay in splintered ruins, their straw scattered across the dilapidated landscape. The cobblestones, which had once echoed with the sounds of laughter and daily life, were eerily silent and empty.

As Jeanette cautiously made her way deeper into the town, she caught glimpses of movement in the shadows. Misshapen creatures, their eyes glowing with an unholy crimson, were barely recognisable as the townspeople she once knew. As they scurried for cover in darkened corners and alleyways, their distorted forms and furtive movements were a stark reminder of the curse that had befallen Millbrook.

The air grew thicker and more oppressive as Jeanette approached the town square. It was there that she saw them: two figures radiating immense power. The vampire stood resplendent in his dark majesty, his presence a black hole of sinister intention that threatened to devour everything in its path. Opposite him, the reaper cut an equally imposing figure, her midnight-black hair whipping around her in an otherworldly wind that seemed to exist solely in her immediate vicinity.

Jeanette's breath caught in her throat as she felt the hatred emanating from both beings – a palpable force, seething and roiling between them with an intensity that made the air crackle. She recognised this animosity as the fruit of her and Heidi's spell; The Puppeteer's Gambit had worked beyond her wildest expectations, brewing a fatal antagonism between the vampire and the reaper.

The vampire's voice cut through the oppressive atmosphere, carrying a resonance that made Jeanette shudder:

"You dare challenge me, reaper?" he said with a snarl, his words dripping with centuries of arrogance and malice. "This town is mine!"

The reaper laughed, but it was a sound so cold and brittle it seemed to freeze the air.

"Your arrogance blinds you, leech," she retorted, her voice ringing with grim finality. "Your reign ends here!"

What happened next was beyond anything Jeanette could have imagined. With a roar that shook even the foundations of the town, the vampire launched himself at the reaper. His movement was a blur of preternatural speed, clawed hands raking across the reaper's ethereal form. Where his attacks landed, they drew not blood, but wisps of darkness, as though he was tearing at the very essence of death itself.

The reaper was far from defenceless. In a burst of cold light, her scythe materialised in her hands. The weapon moved with deadly precision, slicing through the air with a keening wail that set Jeanette's teeth on edge. Each swing left trails of ghostly afterimages, as if the scythe was cutting through more than just physical space.

Jeanette watched in equal parts awe and terror as the two supernatural beings clashed again and again. The vampire's speed was breathtaking, his form little more than a dark smear as he darted in to land vicious blows. But the reaper was implacable, her form dissipating into mist whenever the vampire's attacks seemed to connect, only to reform moments later, unharmed and unrelenting.

As the battle raged on, the town square began to crumble around them. Buildings that had withstood centuries collapsed under the force of their confrontation, reduced to rubble in mere moments. The ground cracked and heaved beneath their feet, fissures spreading out like a spider web from the epicentre of their clash.

Just when it seemed the fight might go on

forever, a turning point arrived. The vampire, in a burst of speed that defied comprehension, managed to disarm the reaper. Her scythe went spinning away, disappearing in a flash of harsh light. For a brief moment, victory gleamed in the vampire's darkened eyes, his lips curling back in a triumphant snarl.

But he had underestimated his foe. The reaper, far from defeated, began to change. Her form expanded, losing definition as it grew, becoming a whirling vortex of shadows that engulfed the vampire. His triumphant expression turned to one of shock and then terror as the reaper's essence began to tear him apart.

The vampire's screams of rage quickly turned into woeful moans of agony, yet even in his final moments, he remained a formidable enemy. As his form disintegrated, he lashed out with the last vestiges of his power. A blast of necrotic energy erupted from his dissolving form, catching the reaper at her very core.

The resulting explosion was cataclysmic. Jeanette was sent tumbling back, momentarily blinded by the intensity of the paranormal force. The sound was deafening, a cacophony of otherworldly energies colliding and annihilating each other. For several long moments, she could do nothing but curl into herself, shielding her eyes and ears from the overwhelming assault on her senses.

When she finally managed to look up again, the scene before her was one of eerie stillness. The town square, which moments ago had been a battlefield of staggering proportions, was now deathly quiet. Where the vampire and reaper had fought, locked in their titanic struggle, there was now nothing but a scorched crater. Wisps of dark energy, the last remnants of their power, dissipated into the air like smoke.

As a strange sense of normality seemed to reassert itself, Jeanette realised the enormity of what had just occurred. The vampire and the reaper, two immensely powerful beings who had seemed invincible, had utterly destroyed each other.

Chapter Fourteen

As the dust settled in the wake of the phenomenal battle, Jeanette found herself standing amidst a crowd of stunned onlookers. The town square now buzzed with a mixture of fear, awe, and tentative hope. Jeanette's heart raced as she scanned the familiar faces surrounding her – faces that had once been contorted with anger and accusation as they had chased her from her home. Now, to her immense relief, no one seemed to notice her; their attention remained fixed on the scorched crater where the vampire and reaper had met their mutual demise.

Jeanette shifted uncomfortably, acutely aware of her precarious position. She was a witch among those who had once feared and reviled her, standing at the crossroads of her past and an uncertain future. As she weighed her options, trying to decide her next move in this delicate situation, a figure moving through the crowd caught her eye.

Her heart nearly stopped.

It was Heidi.

Jeanette blinked rapidly, certain she was hallucinating. Heidi belonged to the realm of the abandoned library, a place she thought she had left behind forever. Yet here was the blonde witch, making her way through the throng of townspeople with purpose, her eyes locked on Jeanette.

As Heidi approached, Jeanette felt a surge of conflicting emotions – joy at seeing her friend again, confusion at her presence beyond the realm to which she belonged, and a touch of apprehension about what her appearance might mean. Before Jeanette could gather her thoughts to speak, Heidi's face broke into a wide smile.

"It worked!" Heidi exclaimed, her voice carrying clearly over the murmur of the crowd. "The Puppeteer's Gambit – it actually worked! Did you see how they tore each other apart?"

Jeanette's eyes widened in alarm as she realised Heidi's words had caught the attention of people nearby. Heads turned in their direction, expressions of curiosity and suspicion replacing the shock of moments before.

Heidi, however, seemed to take this newfound attention in her stride. Her eyes glinted with a confidence Jeanette had never seen in her before.

"Listen, all of you," Heidi began, raising her voice to address the gathering crowd. "There's something you need to know about what just happened here. Jeanette is not the one who cursed your town. In fact, she's the reason you're all free now."

Murmurs of disbelief and confusion, punctuated by sharp gasps of recognition, rippled all around as more people turned to look at Jeanette.

"That vampire was the true source of the curse," Heidi continued, undeterred. "And that reaper? She wanted to manipulate the situation for her own gain. Jeanette and I cast a spell – The Puppeteer's Gambit – to turn them against each other. What you just witnessed was the result of our magic, saving your town and your lives."

The crowd's reaction was a blend of horror, scepticism, and dawning realisation. Some faces showed lingering doubt, while others began to soften with the first hints of remorse. Sensing the pivotal nature of this moment, Heidi made a sweeping gesture with her arm.

"If you don't believe me, just look around you," she challenged. "The curse is breaking even as we speak."

As if on cue, gasps of astonishment swept through the crowd. The misshapen, monstrous forms that had once been townspeople began to shift and change. Grotesque features melted away to be replaced by familiar human visages. The very air seemed to lighten, the oppressive miasma of the curse dissipating like smoke caught in a cleansing breeze.

The transformation was as beautiful as it was unsettling. Jeanette watched in amazement as friends and neighbours she had known all her life emerged from their cursed states, blinking in bewilderment and relief. The proof of Heidi's words was undeniable, written in the very flesh of the townsfolk.

A hush fell over the square as the full impact of what had transpired began to sink in. Then, hesitantly at first but with growing conviction, voices began to rise in apology.

"We're so sorry, Jeanette."

"We were wrong to accuse you."

"Can you ever forgive us for what we did?"

The words washed over Jeanette like a bittersweet tide. The vindication she had longed for was finally here, but the memory of their rejection still stung. Taking a deep breath, she addressed her former persecutors.

"Of course it will take time to heal from what happened," Jeanette said, her voice steady despite the emotion threatening to overwhelm her. "I won't pretend that your actions didn't hurt me deeply, but I don't want to hold on to that pain forever. We've all suffered under this curse, and now we have a chance to move forward together."

She took a long pause, and then gestured to Heidi.

"It wasn't just me who saved you. Heidi also deserves recognition. Without her help, none of this would have been possible."

"I just did what needed to be done," Heidi murmured, tilting her head modestly.

As the crowd began to disperse, breaking into small groups to process the momentous events they had witnessed, Jeanette and Heidi finally found themselves alone. Jeanette turned to her friend, a thousand questions pressing at the edges of her mind.

"Heidi, I... I still can't believe you're here," she said. "How is this possible? I thought I'd never see you again."

Heidi's expression softened, a blend of joy and sadness playing across her features.

"I cast a realm-breaking spell," she explained. "It's not something that can be done lightly or often – the potential for chaos between realms is too great. But I had to see for myself that the Puppeteer's Gambit spell had worked. More than that though, I needed to know that you were safe."

"You risked so much," Jeanette said, worried but touched by Heidi's dedication and loyalty.

"Of course," said Heidi. "But I'd do it again and a thousand times over. You're my friend, Jeanette. More than that, you showed me what I'm capable of. I couldn't just sit in that library, wondering if you'd succeeded or..."

Unable to voice the alternative, Heidi trailed off. It was then that a difficult realisation dawned on Jeanette.

"This is goodbye, isn't it? For real this time."

"It has to be," Heidi confirmed gently, sad but honest. "I can't make a habit of crossing between realms. It's too dangerous."

Jeanette felt tears welling up in her eyes, but she forced them back. She wholeheartedly took Heidi's hands in her own, squeezing them tightly.

"Heidi, listen to me. You are an incredible witch. The confidence you've gained, the power you've shown: you deserve to hold your head high. That academy you want to attend? They'll be lucky to have you."

A spark of pride ignited in Heidi's eyes, so different from the self-doubt she had displayed when Jeanette had first encountered her in the abandoned library.

"Thank you, Jeanette. For everything. I never thought I'd be capable of what we've accomplished."

As they embraced for the last time, Jeanette tried to memorise every detail – the warmth of Heidi's hug, the scent of old books and magic that clung to her, the feeling of having a true friend who understood her completely.

When they finally separated, both women had tears in their eyes. Heidi took a step back, her form already seeming slightly less substantial.

"Goodbye, Jeanette. Take care of yourself, and this town. They're lucky to have you."

Her heart heavy but full, Jeanette watched as

Heidi turned and walked away. When Heidi rounded a corner and disappeared from sight, Jeanette knew she was truly gone – back to the realm of the abandoned library, never to be seen again in this world.

Tears fell freely down Jeanette's cheeks as she stood there, marvelling at the profound impact Heidi had made on her life in such a short time. She felt a complex mixture of emotions – grief at the loss, gratitude for the friendship, and wonder at the incredible journey they had shared.

Distracting Jeanette from her reverie, a small group of townsfolk approached her hesitantly. Their faces were kind now, etched with remorse and newfound respect.

"Jeanette?" one of them ventured. "We'd like to talk, if that's alright – about moving forward. We are in your debt."

Wiping her eyes, Jeanette nodded slowly, a quiet resolve settling over her. The curse was over, the evil vanquished. She had proven her innocence and saved the town. While the road ahead would not be easy, there was now hope – hope for recovery, for redemption, for peace.

www.ingramcontent.com/pod-product-compliance
Lightning Source LLC
Chambersburg PA
CBHW032018180726
48283CB00008B/2731